Catch the Sun

ISBN 978-1-59298-983-6

Library of Congress Catalog Number: 2013907463
Printed in the United States of America
Fifth Printing: 2019

22 21 20 19   8 7 6 5

Story by Anne Johnson
Illustrations by Shawn McCann
Book design by Mayfly Design

BEAVER'S POND
PRESS

7108 Ohms Lane
Edina, Minnesota 55439
(952) 829-8818
www.BeaversPondPress.com

To order, visit www.itascabooks.com
or call 1-800-901-3480. Reseller discounts available.

Mortenson | Renewable Energy Groups

Mortenson Construction would like to thank Beavers Pond Press and the design team for the hard work and seamless collaboration that went into producing this book.

10% Post-consumer waste

Fresh Ideas

Did you know that North America—specifically the southwestern states of the USA—is one of the best places in the world for producing **energy** from the sun? Special equipment turns the rays of sunlight that brighten your day into solar energy. Even in parts of North America that don't soak up so much sun, such as some Canadian provinces, homes and businesses have started collecting the sun's energy.

Solar energy is part of the solution for a cleaner energy future. As a source of energy, sunlight is free, its supplies are unlimited, and it is available almost everywhere in the world. This book will introduce you to solar energy and give you an idea of what it takes to build a solar energy project.

Knowledge is power, so seize the opportunity and catch the sun!

The faucet squeaked as Nels turned it on and water began filling his small pool. Nels wasn't swimming today. He was testing his first solar-powered boat.

It was the perfect day to try out his boat. Not only was the sun shining brightly in the afternoon sky, it was also the day his father was coming home from a long work trip. Just as Nels set the boat in the water, he heard his father's truck pull up.

Bright Idea

On a clear, sunny day, the earth receives about 1,000 **watts** of solar energy per square meter. That's like placing ten 100-watt light bulbs in a 3-foot-square box!

Nels and his father watched the boat sail across the pool.

"Look, Dad! The sun is powering my boat," exclaimed Nels. "I used the solar-power kit that you gave me for my birthday!"

"Nels, this is really great!" said his dad. "You know, over the next few weeks I'll need to visit different construction projects for work. Lots of them use **clean energy** from the sun. Would you like to come with me while you're on summer break?"

"You mean a solar project tour?" Nels said. "That would be great!" He was thrilled to have the chance to see solar energy at work on a MUCH larger scale.

7

Nels searched the Internet to learn about solar power before his trip.

He found out that the sun sends out a huge amount of energy every day. Like other stars, the sun is a giant ball of gas—mostly hydrogen and helium. As these gases are formed, the sun produces energy. This radiant energy is known as **solar energy**.

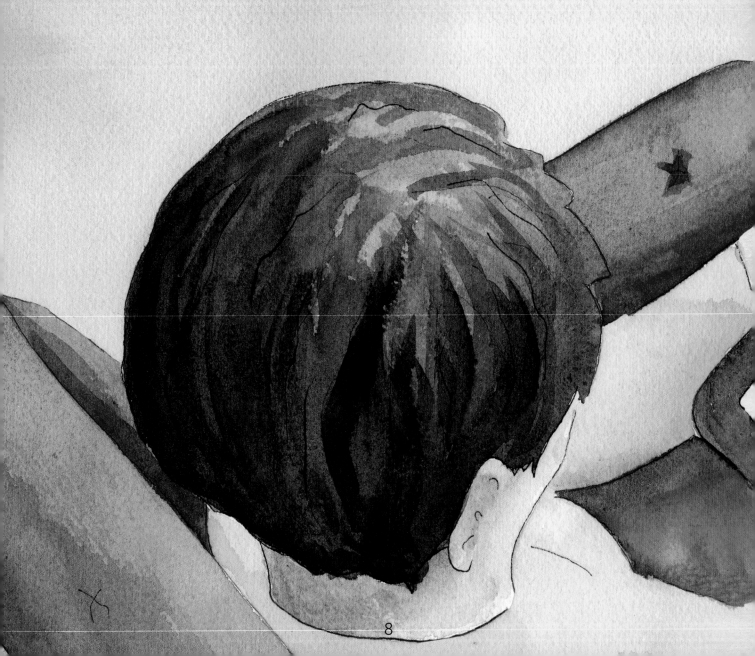

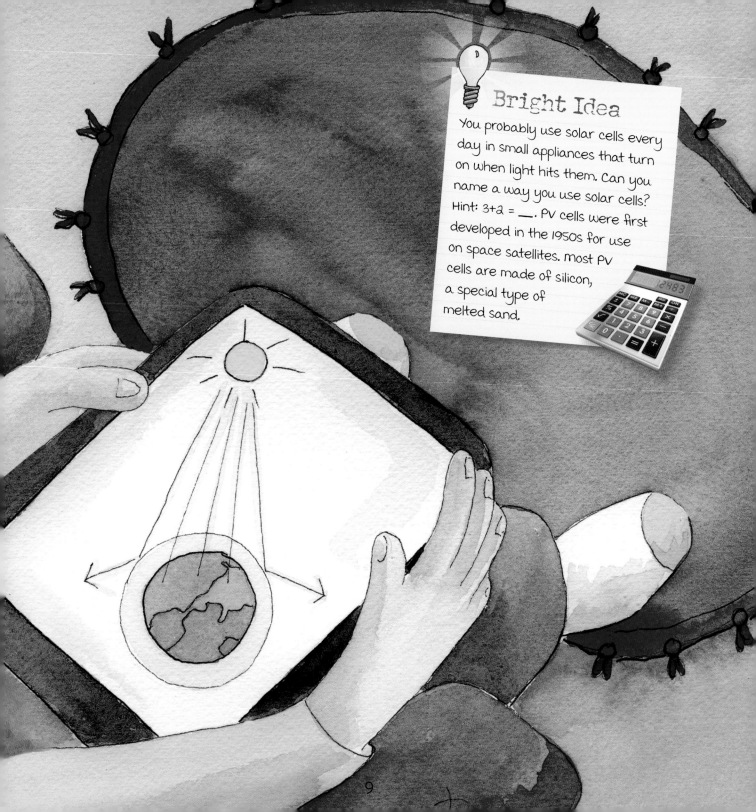

The sun is our nearest star. Without it, life would not exist on our planet. It is crucial to our survival, and we rely on it each day in many ways. Because the sun shines on us every day, solar energy is a renewable source of energy. **Renewable energy** is energy from a source that is naturally replenished, or renewed—like the sun.

SUN

Bright Idea

Solar energy is stored in plant matter and is responsible for powering the water cycle and producing wind. Even oil and natural gas are the result of solar energy. They were formed from plants and animals that lived thousands of years ago.

The sun provides energy to plants as well. Sunlight powers **photosynthesis**, the chemical process that converts carbon dioxide into sugars, which plants use as food.

Nels could picture this food chain beginning with the sun. Plants need the sun's light to grow. Animals eat plants for their food. Humans eat plants and animals.

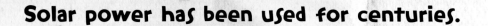

Solar power has been used for centuries.

WORSHIPPED BY THE ANCIENTS

As far back as five thousand years ago, people worshipped the sun. Ra, the sun god, was considered the first king of Egypt. In Greece there were two sun gods, Apollo and Helios.

LIGHTING FIRES

As early as 300 BC, Greeks and Romans used tools called burning mirrors to focus the sun's heat and light fires.

TELLING TIME

The sundial is a device that measures time by the position of the sun. The sun shines on a thin rod, casting a shadow onto a surface marked with lines indicating the hours of the day. The earliest sundials we know about are from Egypt, around 3500 BC. Today you can often find sundials decorating gardens.

DRYING CLOTHES

When we hang laundry outside, we are using the sun's heat to dry our clothes. Humans have probably done so for as long as they've worn clothes!

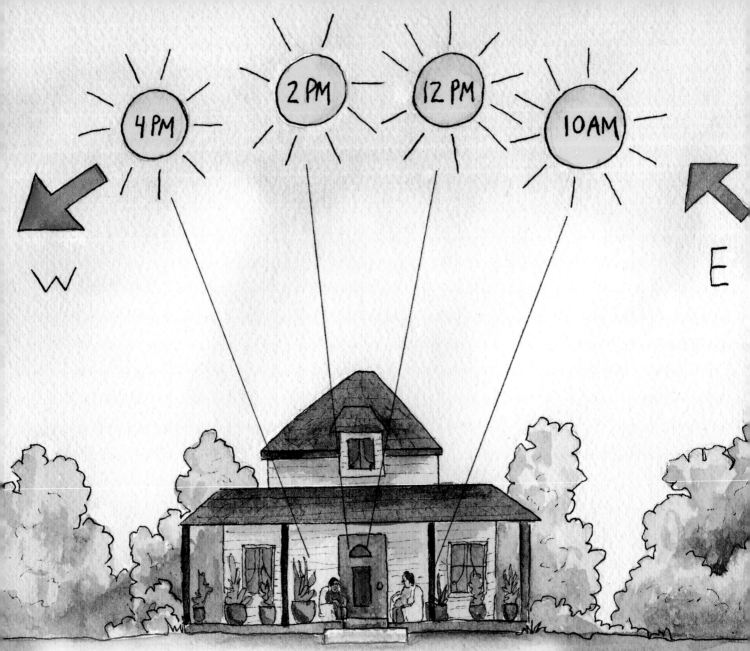

The morning of their trip, Nels's father called him out onto the sun porch.

"Let's have breakfast here," he said. The porch was warm in the sunshine.

"The windows face south to capture more sun, especially in winter," his father explained. "The sun rises in the east and sets in the west, and in Minnesota, the sun sits lower in the sky during winter. So we know that the south side of the house will always get more sun."

EQUATOR

N

W

S

E

💡 Bright Idea

In the northern hemisphere, windows that face the south get the most heat from the sun. In the southern hemisphere, it is the opposite: north-facing windows get more sun. Do you know why? Use a thermometer to record the temperatures in different rooms of your home. Pay attention to the direction their windows face.

Nels's father explained that they were going to visit two different solar energy construction projects. However, Nels learned that there are far more than two ways to catch the rays of the sun and create power! Explore and compare a few of these different technologies. What is similar? What is different?

Solar Trough: Curved rows of mirrors focus sunlight on a tube filled with heat-sensitive liquid. As it heats up, that liquid expands and moves through a steam generator to produce electricity. The mirrors move during the day to follow the sun and reflect the most sunlight.

Solar Power Tower: Large, sun-tracking mirrors focus sunlight on a receiver at the top of a tower. The receiver is full of fluid. When it heats up, it turns into steam. A **generator** uses the steam to produce electricity.

PV Solar: Photovoltaic (PV) cells convert sunlight directly into electricity. A **module** is a group of PV cells connected electrically and fitted into a frame known as a solar panel. These panels can sit in an angled frame that does not move (fixed) or in one that moves to follow the path of the sun (tracked).

There are other ways to gather solar energy. Visit the library or use the Internet to find out about other types of solar technology. Here are some clues to get you started: research solar heating systems, solar thermal energy, and solar electricity.

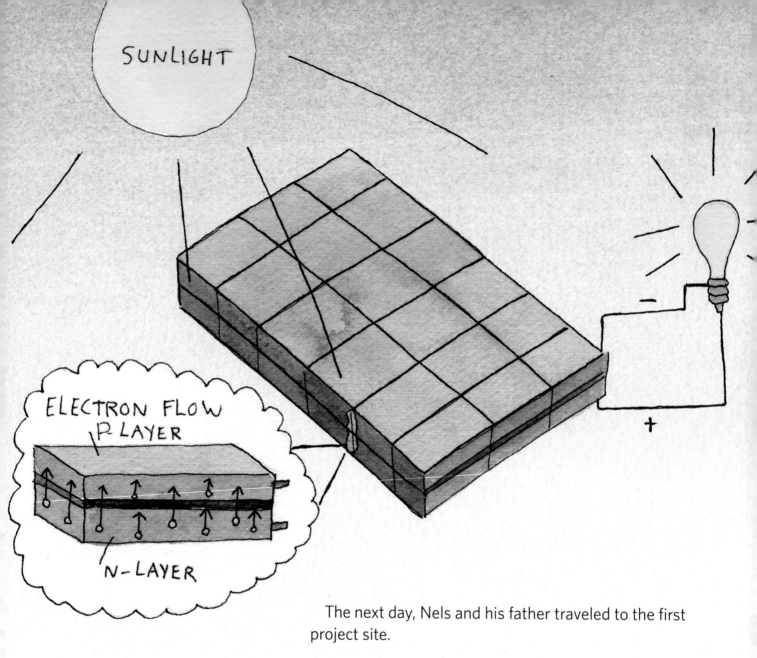

The next day, Nels and his father traveled to the first project site.

His father said, "The project we're going to visit today is a photovoltaic solar plant.

"A PV solar plant produces energy using cells just like the ones in your solar boat. When sunlight strikes the solar cell, tiny particles called **electrons** are knocked loose. The movement of the electrons through the solar cell creates an electrical **current**."

18

Nels's father took out a map of the project to show him how the site would look when it was finished. He pointed to the rows shown on the map.

He said, "This is where the PV modules will go. A group of PV modules is called an **array**. Some of the arrays are set on special tracking devices to follow the sun as it moves through the sky."

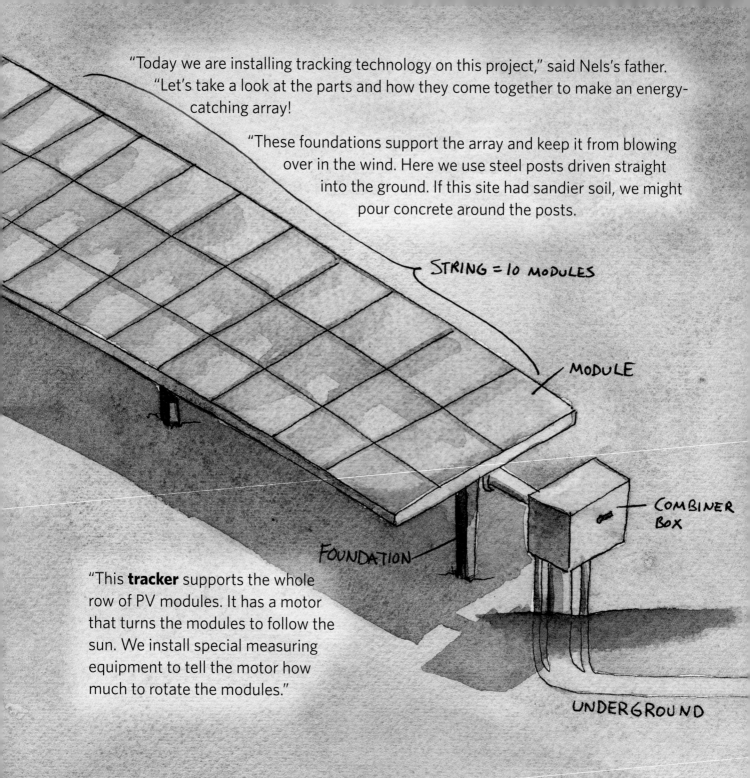

"Today we are installing tracking technology on this project," said Nels's father. "Let's take a look at the parts and how they come together to make an energy-catching array!

"These foundations support the array and keep it from blowing over in the wind. Here we use steel posts driven straight into the ground. If this site had sandier soil, we might pour concrete around the posts.

STRING = 10 MODULES

MODULE

COMBINER BOX

FOUNDATION

"This **tracker** supports the whole row of PV modules. It has a motor that turns the modules to follow the sun. We install special measuring equipment to tell the motor how much to rotate the modules."

UNDERGROUND

"These solar modules convert the sun's light into energy. The wires that connect module to module transfer the electricity down the row. Only a handful of modules are connected together. This is called a **string**.

"Many strings are combined into larger wires at a **combiner box**. The largest wires are buried underground to make their way to a power station.

"The power station converts the power from DC (**direct current**) to AC (**alternating current**) using an **inverter**."

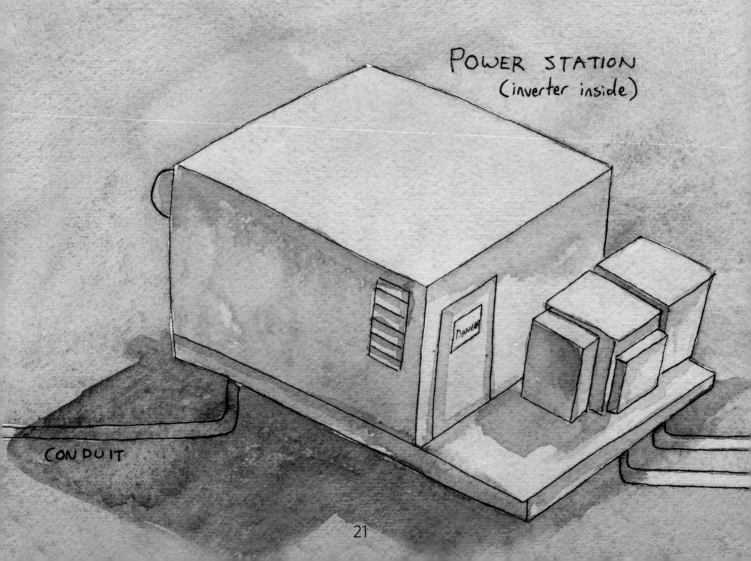

POWER STATION
(inverter inside)

CONDUIT

"Now that you can identify the equipment found on a PV solar farm, let's follow the steps to build the facility."

1. First, workers clear and level the site. When the site is ready, roads are built to each power station. A fence may be built to protect the electrical equipment and to keep people safe.
2. Workers install the post foundations.

3. When the foundations are ready, workers weld or bolt the tracking system together. Most parts of the tracking system are light enough that workers can lift them into place. Some of the heavier pieces are lifted by a small skid steer or forklift.
4. Once the tracker is up, workers install the solar modules.
5. Electricians follow behind and wire the modules together to form strings.

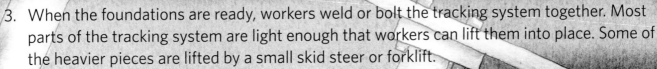

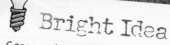

Bright Idea

Some solar projects operate in snowy areas of the country. A big snowdrift is very heavy! Engineers have designed support structures that are strong enough to hold not only the solar modules, but also the extra weight of heavy snow.

6. Other crews of electricians dig trenches and lay cable in the ground along the tracker rows.
7. The cables connect the modules to the power station, which will either be built at the site or delivered by truck and lowered into place by a crane.

Finally, the electricians connect each power station to the next using the underground cable. Together, the cables send the power to an onsite **substation**, which connects the solar facility to the **grid** that delivers electricity to your home.

Bright Idea

The solar field must be grounded. Copper cables run from the equipment into the ground. Grounding protects equipment from power surges by directing these big bursts of energy into the earth. What natural phenomenon might cause sudden bursts of electricity outdoors?

Solar projects can be hot places to work! Nels got a drink of water in the shady area where the workers take their breaks. His father told him that the crew had begun their work very early in the morning, so that their workday would be done before the hottest part of the day. Do you see other ways workers are being protected?

Soon it was time for Nels and his father to move to the next site.

"Next, we're going to visit a site where we are using **concentrated solar power**," said Nels's father. "Many parts of the process will look similar, but the equipment is much larger!"

When they got to the site, Nels saw the difference right away. This site used Mega-Modules, which are 77 feet long by 49 feet wide. They cover more ground than some houses!

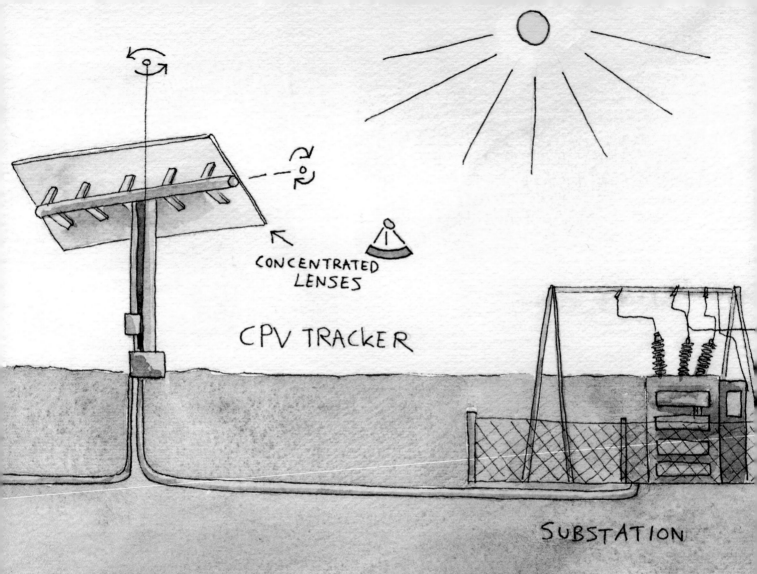

CONCENTRATED
LENSES

CPV TRACKER

SUBSTATION

Concentrated Photovoltaic (CPV) technology focuses large amounts of sunlight onto small photovoltaic surfaces to generate electricity. CPV systems have special trackers that move both up and down and side to side as they track the sun. They are called dual-**axis** trackers because they track the sun along two different lines.

"Because the Mega-Modules are much larger than the other PV modules we saw, the foundations must be larger, too. And we need larger cranes to install the CPV trackers."

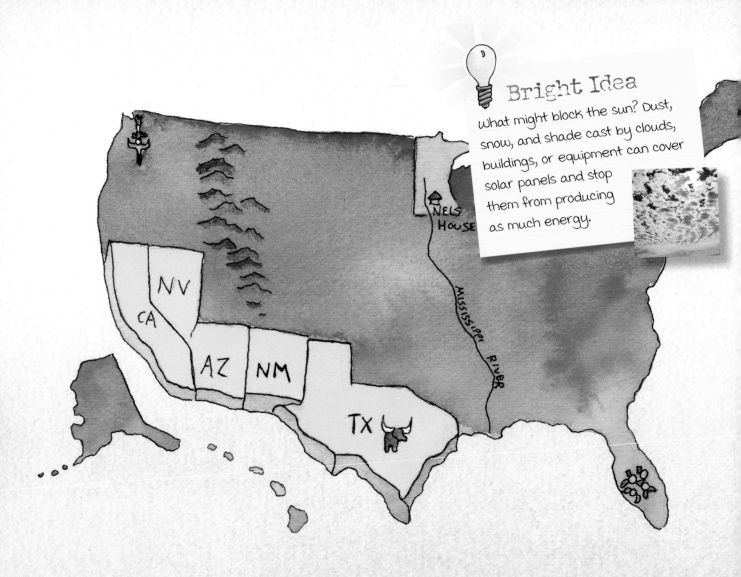

Bright Idea

What might block the sun? Dust, snow, and shade cast by clouds, buildings, or equipment can cover solar panels and stop them from producing as much energy.

Nels remembered that some areas in North America are better solar resources than others. According to the National Weather Service, the five sunniest states are Arizona, California, Nevada, New Mexico, and Texas.

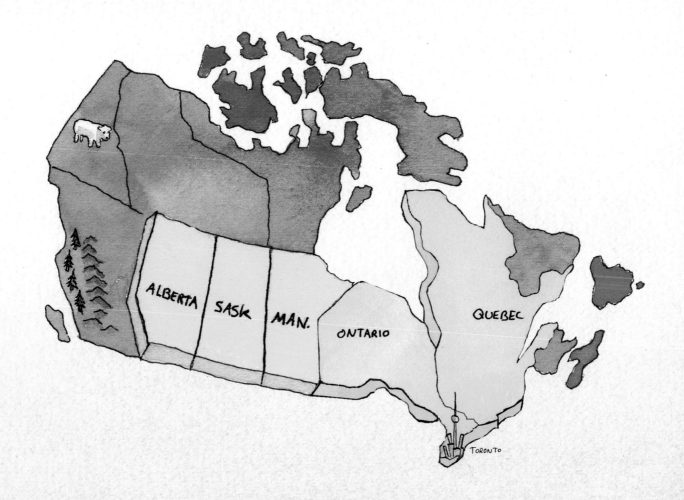

According to the Centre for Energy, the sunniest areas of Canada are southern Ontario, Quebec, and the prairies of Alberta, Saskatchewan, and Manitoba.

The northern territories have less direct sunlight because they are far from the equator. However, some northern towns receive twenty-four hours of daylight in one day during the summer—the sun never goes down! That makes up for the winter, when there are days with twenty-four hours of darkness.

As they ended their visit, Nels's father explained, "Solar energy facilities aren't just good for the environment. They're also good for communities. Solar farms need people to manage the facilities and to keep the modules clean and the equipment operating correctly. And the solar industry creates lots of other jobs, too."

ENVIRONMENTAL and **CIVIL ENGINEERS** make sure the site is right for the project and help protect native plants and animals.

LAWYERS put together contracts between landowners and solar developers.

TRANSPORTATION COMPANIES ship the materials to the site.

ENGINEERS design solar energy equipment, foundations, and electrical systems.

And **CONSTRUCTION WORKERS** build the solar energy facilities.

MANUFACTURERS produce the solar modules and other pieces of equipment.

"Solar energy is not just for large installations. People can install smaller systems at their homes and businesses. Some of them aren't much more complicated than your solar-powered boat. For example, the sun's rays can power water heaters, parking structures, garden lights, emergency phones, and even streetlights."

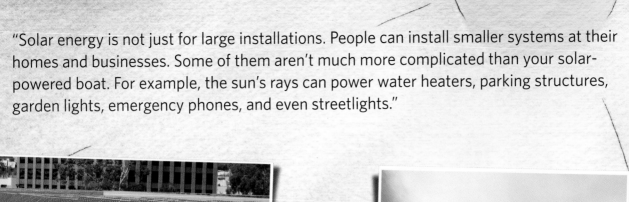

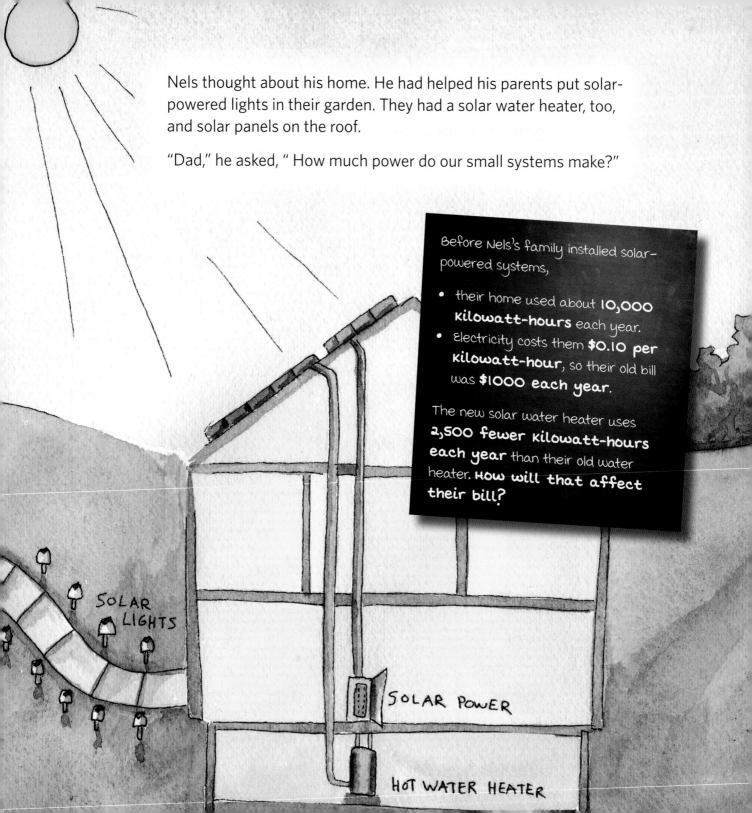

Nels thought about his home. He had helped his parents put solar-powered lights in their garden. They had a solar water heater, too, and solar panels on the roof.

"Dad," he asked, " How much power do our small systems make?"

Before Nels's family installed solar-powered systems,

- their home used about **10,000 kilowatt-hours** each year.
- Electricity costs them **$0.10 per kilowatt-hour**, so their old bill was **$1000 each year.**

The new solar water heater uses **2,500 fewer kilowatt-hours each year** than their old water heater. **How will that affect their bill?**

SOLAR LIGHTS

SOLAR POWER

HOT WATER HEATER

After learning about the power of the sun, Nels was proud that his father worked to build **renewable energy**. He wondered what other things his community was doing to save energy. Have you investigated your community lately?

Glossary

alternating current (AC) - an electric current that regularly reverses direction

array - a connected group of PV solar modules

axis - an imaginary straight line around which an object rotates

clean energy – energy that does not create pollution when used

combiner box – the point at which many module strings are combined into larger wires on the way to a power station

concentrated solar power - a way of making solar power by focusing large amounts of sunlight onto small, high-efficiency photovoltaic surfaces to generate electricity

current - the flow of an electric charge

direct current (DC) - electrical current that flows in only one direction

electron – a negatively charged particle of electricity

energy - power, especially power that comes from sources such as fossil fuel, electricity, or solar radiation

fossil fuel - a combustible material, such as oil, coal, or natural gas, formed in the earth from plant or animal remains

generator - a machine that converts one form of energy into another

grid - a network of power lines or pipelines used to move energy from its source to consumers

inverter - an electrical power converter that changes direct current (DC) to alternating current (AC)

kilowatt - a unit of electric demand equal to 1,000 watts

kilowatt-hour - A unit of energy equal to 1,000 watt-hours; a measure of electricity energy generation or use

megawatt - equal to 1,000 kilowatts or 1 million watts

module - a group of photovoltaic cells connected electrically and fitted together into a solar panel

non-renewable energy - energy taken from finite resources, such as fossil fuels

photosynthesis - the chemical process by which plants convert carbon dioxide into the sugars they use for food

photovoltaic (PV) - able to produce electric current using light

renewable energy - any naturally occurring source of energy that is not likely to run out, such as biomass, solar, wind, tidal, wave, and hydroelectric power

solar cell - an electrical device that converts the energy of light directly into electricity (also called a photovoltaic cell)

solar energy - energy gathered from the sun's radiation

string – a small number of modules connected by wires that transfer electricity to a central cable

substation - a power station where electrical current is converted to an easily usable form

tracker - a structure that moves to follow, or track, the path of the sun

watt – the basic unit of electrical power

Sources Consulted

Centre for Energy
KidWind.org
NEED Project Curriculum
U.S. Department of Energy, National Renewable Energy Lab
U.S. National Weather Service

Further Reading

To learn more about solar energy, visit these very informative websites!

CanSIA
http://www.cansia.ca

Centre for Energy
http://www.centreforenergy.com/education

Database of State Initiatives for Renewables and Efficiency (DSIRE)
http://www.dsireusa.org

Department of Renewable Energy: Energy Efficiency and Renewable Energy
http://www.eere.energy.gov/kids

Energy Quest
http://www.energyquest.ca.gov

Kidwind Project
http://www.kidwind.org

Solar Energy Industries Association
http://www SEIA.org

TREC Renewable Energy Co-operative
http://www.trec.on.ca

Photo Credits

Mortenson would like to thank the members of its project teams whose photographs appear throughout the book, as well as the following organizations:

E.ON Climate & Renewables
Alamosa Solar Facility, owned and operated by Cogentrix
GE Power and Water
Photographer, Dennis Schwartz